TALES OF HEAVEN AND EARTH

Hyacinthe Vulliez
is a journalist and writer
who knows Africa well, having
lived and worked there for many years.

Cover design by Peter Bennett

Published by Creative Education
123 South Broad Street, Mankato, Minnesota 56001
Creative Education is an imprint
of The Creative Company

Library of Congress Cataloging-in-Publication Data

Vulliez, Hyacinthe.
[Les secrets de Kaidara. English]
The secrets of Kaidara / by Hyacinthe Vulliez;
illustrated by Etienne Souppart;
translated by Gwen Marsh.
p. cm. — (Tales of heaven and earth)
Summary: Three men set out on a difficult journey to find the
secrets of the mystical country of Kaidara. Explanatory sidebars reveal
the animist beliefs of the Peuls, or Fula, of West Africa.
ISBN 0-88682-823-6

1. Fula (African people)—Folklore. 2. Folklore—Africa, West.
I. Souppart Etienne, ill. II. Marsh, Gwen. III. Title. IV. Series.
PZ8.1.V84Se   1997
398.2'089'96322—dc20   96-30902

6 5 4 3 2 1

THE
SECRETS
OF KAIDARA

BY HYACINTHE VULLIEZ
ILLUSTRATED BY ETIENNE SOUPPART
TRANSLATED BY GWEN MARSH

CREATIVE EDUCATION

We are in the land of the Peul herdsmen.

The Peuls live in West Africa, in the countries of Mali and Niger. Their skin is copper or black. They herd cattle and sheep. Originally nomads, they now settle in villages. They love secrets— anything that has a hidden meaning. Another name for them is *Fulbes*. (See map on page 33.)

This story comes from the vast land of the Peuls, in Africa. Here villagers build their huts close together for protection against wild animals and the fierce sun. Beyond lies the steppe, where only short, thorny plants grow, and beyond that is the desert with its red sand dunes, mountains of black stones, and wadis that swell in the rains. In one of these villages lived three boys who were inseparable friends: Demburu, Hamtudo, and Hammadi. This was long ago

Wadis are rivers that flood suddenly in the rainy season. As soon as the rain stops they dry up.

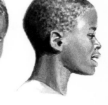

The One-eyed King is the Sun; thanks to his one eye, he can see everything that happens on Earth. His fierce gaze was enough to harden mountains that were too soft when the world began. Africans are, by tradition, animists. For them all beings, whether animate or not, possess a spirit, and certain stars, rivers, and trees are gods.

The three friends offer a sacrifice to the Great God, Gueno, so that their journey may go well. The sacrifice is an offering (of animals and fruits) to the gods to win their goodwill.

when the One-eyed King, the Sun, was still hardening the mountains and genies were digging the riverbeds.

One day the three friends decided to look for the land of Kaidara, which was so far away that no one knew where it lay. Before setting out they went hunting. They lit a big fire and threw the game they had caught onto it as an offering to the gods. As the flames died, a hole opened at their feet, and they saw a stairway leading down into the earth. They decided to follow it and found three oxen waiting for them at the bottom, carrying water and provisions of all kinds. Off they went, each driving his ox in front of him. They walked on for a long time, through a forest of tall trees, full of

Genies are invisible beings, who often take the form of very small old men, only a few feet tall. Hence their name, *pygmy-genies,* after the pygmies, the very small race of people who live in equatorial Africa. Genies are extremely powerful.

To descend into the earth means to look for the meaning of things hidden. The stairs are a symbol of the way to knowledge.

In Africa, the chameleon is an animal of the sun, a divine creature.

the sounds of wild animals.

At last, weary and down to their last drop of water, they came upon a wide plain. Just then they saw a giant chameleon, an animal that changes color according to its surroundings. Its swivel eyes can look in all directions. It addressed the travelers in a friendly way. "It's good, very good, to observe things and learn. I am the first sign from the land of the pygmy-genies, but my secret belongs to Kaidara, who is close at hand and far away. Take heart! Continue on your way!" Then the chameleon disappeared.

Toward evening Hamtudo saw a giant bat flying above him. "Look," he cried, "look at that big bird that looks like a genie." Its great flapping wings made a mournful sound. But the bat reassured them. "Don't be afraid! Daylight blinds me but I see clearly at night. I am the second sign from the land of the pygmy-genies. My secret belongs to Kaidara, who is close at hand and far away. Take heart! Go on your way!" The

At last the travelers hear the name of the one they seek: Kaidara, god of gold and knowledge. This god comes close to humans by appearing to them in some form they recognize, but then he disappears and remains far away and inaccessible.

The gods live everywhere: in springs and rivers and trees. They can appear in the form of people or animals.

bat vanished and the three friends were alone again with their oxen. It seemed as if an invisible hand was unrolling the plain ahead of them into infinity. They were terribly thirsty, and the oxen bellowed for water.

The travelers were tired and fell asleep beneath the stars. They slept so deeply all night that they never even heard the hyena prowling about.

At dawn, the hour that scorpions are most active, a large one came toward them with evil intent. Hamtudo took a step toward it, and bowed with hands joined in supplication, "O Scorpion, we don't believe you are wicked. Please help us find water—take pity, we are so thirsty!"

"Take this path," it replied. "Keep straight on without stopping. And recite this prayer: 'O Spirit of the Waters, you who make the rivers invisible in Kaidara's land, show them to us. We are going to Kaidara, who is close

As a nocturnal animal, the bat inspires fear. Like the chameleon, it has good and bad qualities.

The scorpion is also a nocturnal animal, dangerous and very much feared. Some species have a poisonous sting that is deadly. It symbolizes wickedness, but also sacrifice, for it is said that its young feed on its entrails.

at hand and far away.' I am the third sign."

The scorpion disappeared and the boys began to pray. Then they found a pool of water a few yards away. They rushed to it. Pure water to drink! But at the pool poisonous snakes were slipping into the water. The boys drew back, terrified. They threw themselves down under a big kapok tree to rest. "We are dying of thirst," said Hammadi sadly, "and these evil spirits prevent us from drinking." "We are the fourth sign . . ." the snakes hissed. The boys went on without refreshment. Far off they saw a tree whose top was lost in the sky. When they reached it they saw gazelles' hoof prints beneath it—full of water! Hammadi threw himself to the ground and started lapping. As fast as he drank, the hole filled up. They all quenched their thirst. Then they heard a voice, "I am the fifth sign from Kaidara's land, close at hand and far away. Take heart! Go on your way. . . ."

The kapok tree is a very tall tree that grows in tropical regions. It has great buttresses at the base of the trunk.

Spirits are invisible beings, gods. The spirits of Water have the power to make the rivers in Kaidara's land invisible.

Snakes play an important part in all religions. They are often seen as the enemy of humankind. The Peuls give them family names such as Papa Boa, Mother Viper, and Uncle Cobra. For the Peuls, snakes can be benevolent as well as hostile.

Their journey holds many mysteries. Only Kaidara...

The three friends set off again, their thoughts full of the dangers they had escaped. Worn out, thirsty and hungry, discouraged by all these events they did not understand, they decided to stop under a leafy tree. The leaves were even bigger and wider than those of the bread-fruit tree, which are enormous. "We'll feel better in the shade," said Hammadi with a sigh. All three lay down with their faces turned toward the thick foliage, far from the nightmares and frights they had been through. By some miracle, they felt neither hunger nor thirst, and they fell asleep.

The bread-fruit tree grows in tropical regions. It has huge leaves and its fruits are as big as round loaves of bread—hence its name.

. . . will be able to explain them.

As if the giant tree had waited for the moment when their eyes closed, its leaves took flight one by one and settled on the bare branches of a tree nearby. Surprised by the light, the three boys rubbed their eyes. "What is going on?" They looked at one another, amazed. "Our tree hasn't any leaves now. Let's change trees." And Hammadi added, "We're truly in a land of wonders. Only Kaidara can tell us the meaning of all these signs. Why doesn't he do that?"

As he finished speaking, the leaves left the new tree and flew back to the first one. Three times they went back and forth. Then Hammadi cried out: "O great Gueno, all this must surely mean something. Help us to understand!" At that moment, a gorgeous bird flew overhead. Its beak and claws were red, its feathers all colors of the rainbow. These were the words it sang: "You have arrived safely in the heart of the pygmy-genies' village." Then the trees spoke. "We are the sixth sign. Only Kaidara knows the secret. Go on, don't lose heart!"

Gueno is God the Creator, the supreme God, eternal and all powerful. It is he who deals out good and bad.

11

They continue their journey, driven by an invisible force.

Once again they set off, not knowing which way to go. But they kept on walking anyway, until suddenly a wall of dry earth rose up in front of them. There was no door to let them through! They waited there for three days and three nights, not knowing what to do. When they decided to continue, part of the wall crumbled and vanished under the ground. Through the gap in the wall they saw a thatched hut. They decided to go in. A rooster was strutting proudly up and down. As they stepped in further they could make out a figure in a dark corner, a curious old man. Down to his hips he was human, but the rest of his body was a serpent. The boys were terrified. But the mysterious being reassured them. "You are welcome, children," he said gently. "Enter this house in peace. It is mine; it is yours." And they were certainly very well looked after. They ate and they drank. But the rooster suddenly turned into a ram, and

The number three is symbolic in many civilizations. In this story, for example, there are three travelers, three loads of gold, three words of advice . . . Kaidara sneezes three times. The number expresses perfection and completeness.

They are determined, though they don't know which way to go.

For the Peuls, the rooster in the house represents a secret kept in silence. Its transformation into a ram means that the secret has been revealed to those nearest. When it becomes a bull, the secret has been divulged to all the people. Finally, its presence in the bush means the secret has reached the ears of the enemy. This spells ruin.

the ram into a bull, a raging bull that turned everything upside down, charged at everyone with its horns, and finally set fire to the trees and grass in the surrounding bush. "Wherever can we be?" cried Demburu.

The ashes of the fire flickered and answered, "You are coming to a land of wonders." And the old man, who had turned into a white cloud, added, "I, who speak to you, and everything you have seen, we are the seventh sign of the pygmy-genies' country. Our secret belongs to Kaidara who is close at hand and far away. Take heart! Continue on your way."

They walked day and night. Forty days and forty nights. At dawn on the fortieth day they came to a deep valley hemmed in by high mountains. A loud voice proclaimed, "Keep on! Kaidara will reward you."

Forty is the number for a time of waiting and for a time of trials and ordeals.

They arrive in a land of wonders.

Immediately
they came upon a
marvel! The waters of two beautiful springs mingled
above a third which had run dry. All three springs called
out together: "We are the eighth sign."

Once more the three travelers went forward, drawn by
an invisible force. Coming to another valley, they found a
man gathering sticks into a bundle, but it was too heavy
for him to lift. In spite of that, he kept adding more sticks
and trying to lift the load onto his back. In vain—the
bundle fell to the ground. Three times he tried. Demburu
burst out laughing. "This man's a fool." The man
answered, "I keep trying to add more to a
weight that's already enough to crush me. I
know I don't know what I'm doing. But
you, who think you know better, can learn
from me: I am the ninth sign from the land of
the pygmy-genies."

Mysteries deepen. . . .

3

Some spirits are
invisible beings
that can take
human form.

"When shall we see the end of all these adventures, these signs and mysteries?" the three companions wondered. All of a sudden, a metal wall rose up in front of them, as tall as the sky. Then a voice spoke to them. "I am an air spirit. My body is vapor . . . I live in the air. Beware! Keep your voices low from now on. There is a reason why you have seen all these signs. Those who have scorned them have been swallowed up. Many more will die in the same way and for the same reason."

They discovered, almost under their feet, a great, dark

Suddenly there's a dazzling meeting with Kaidara—he who is far away...

To be worthy to see wonders, the three travelers must overcome their fear (the dark hole) and their disgust (the stinking filth), without complaining.

hole full of stinking filth. The next instant, this disgusting hole turned into an elegant room with magnificent carpets and lovely perfumes. Invisible hands set down a golden throne in their midst; a strange being came and sat on it—he had seven heads, twelve arms and thirty feet. It was Kaidara, Kaidara who is close at hand and far away. Speaking for the three of them, Hammadi said, "O Kaidara, for years and years we have been wandering along difficult paths looking for you! Now we are very happy to find you and to hail you as our master."

The seven heads of Kaidara correspond to the seven days of the week, the twelve arms to the twelve months of the year, and the thirty feet to the thirty days in a month.

. . . and close at hand!

Kaidara greeted them with a smile and ordered a pygmy-genie to bring gold, enough for three oxen to carry. Then he gave each of the travelers one of these oxen with its load of gold. It was a fortune! Hammadi, who had come through so many ordeals for answers, not gold, asked quietly, "O great Kaidara, your gold is good, we thank you for it, but above all we would like to know the meaning of the signs we have seen. Only you can enlighten us."

Kaidara was delighted with this request and replied at once, "Use wisely the gold I have given you. It will be the means of your learning all you want to know."

The sun and the turning throne are signs of Kaidara's greatness.

Kaidara seemed to be the center of a dazzling sun, and the throne he sat on was turning constantly. The three friends were enthralled. Hammadi exclaimed excitedly, "I would give all the gold in the world to know the meaning of the nine signs we saw." Then Kaidara gave each of them two more oxen loaded with gold.

The three travelers left this enchanted place in a joyful mood and began the return

journey to their village. As they walked they fell silent, each one thinking about what he would do with his gold.

Suddenly Demburu said, "I'll buy a kingdom with lots of towns and villages and lands. I'll be a king! Yes, a king! And everyone will obey me, fear me, and revere me."

Hamtudo grinned mischievously. "You're a fool," he said. "Kings' lives aren't as happy as you think. They are the most miserable of men, with endless cares and troubles. I shall use my gold to become a trader. I shall buy goods at a low price and sell at a high price, and I shall get richer and richer. All the storytellers will shout my name in the towns and villages: 'Hamtudo is the richest man in the world. He can do anything he pleases and have no worries at all.' "

Hammadi felt sad. He hardly dared say what was on his mind. What will they think of me if I tell them what I am going to do? He hesitated, then came out with his idea: "I don't want to sit on a throne, nor swim in riches. There's only one thing I want—I'll spend everything to find out at last what those signs meant in the land of the pygmy-genies. People will call me an idiot. Let them!

A storyteller, especially in West Africa, where he is called a *griot*, goes from village to village telling stories in words and song. He also brings the latest news.

But I think that knowledge is the only really important thing in a person's life."

Hamtudo and Demburu shrugged their shoulders. They were tolerant and kind, but they didn't understand their friend's obstinacy. How could he think of giving up everything just for the sake of having those mysteries explained? For them, the wealth Kaidara had given them was already the key to happiness.

The three friends traveled on, driving their oxen before them with their loads of gold.

4

An old man was sitting on the bough of a huge bread-fruit tree, staring at the sky and the stars. His clothes were in rags and he was covered with lice. Hamtudo and Demburu burst out laughing. "That fellow's a madman!" they cried. Hammadi, on the other hand, greeted him politely, asking after his health and his family, as is the custom in Africa. Then he picked the lice off him, helped him to tidy up a bit, and gave him a gentle massage. "Would you do something that would give me great pleasure?" he asked, and then went on, "Accept this gold. You will be able to buy food for yourself and clothes to wear." The old

In many African cultures, great age is venerated, and old people are especially respected for their wisdom.

man replied at once, "A thousand thanks, you are kind, but I can't accept. Besides, you know, I can spend days and nights without eating or drinking. Any moment now the star will appear and I'll have to leave you and go to Kaidara who is far away and close at hand." Hammadi's eyes lit up, "If you are going to Kaidara's land, give me some advice. I shall treasure it."

"I'll be glad to give you one piece of advice to start with," answered the old man, "but on one condition— you must pay me!"

Hammadi was surprised. Pay for advice? Well, if that was what he had to do for a happy life! "I'll give you one of these three oxen loaded with gold," he said.

"Loaded with gold? But what have you done to obtain this gold?"

"It was Kaidara the Marvelous; he gave it to me."

The old man asks to be paid for his advice, not for love of money, but to put Hammadi to the test: one comes to wisdom only at the cost of much effort and patience.

. . . Hammadi is prepared to give away all his gold.

"In that case, this is my advice: never travel at night in the season of rain and storms!"

"Thank you. I'll do as you say. But can you give me some more advice?"

"Yes, but can you pay me?"

"I'll give you another ox with its load of gold," replied Hammadi without hesitating.

The old man smiled at him in silence. Then he said, "This is my second piece of advice: never offend against our ancestors' customs; respect our ancient taboos."

Hammadi thought about this for a long time, as though listening to an inner voice, then he said, "Agreed. But if you could give me one more piece of advice as to how to make a success of my life. . . ."

"Can you pay for advice a third time?"

Would Hammadi part with the third ox, his last one, and its load of gold? He stroked the animal and looked at its burden. At last he came to a decision and said to the old man, "I'll give you my last ox." The man burst out laughing, sneezed three times, and great tears ran down his cheeks into his beard. He nodded, stood silent for a time,

Customs are very important to African peoples. Customs regulate their lives and act as laws.

The old man laughs and cries, a sign that he is greatly moved by Hammadi's offer of his entire fortune in exchange for three pieces of advice.

Taboos are rules that forbid certain things. Breaking such rules is often punished by the gods.

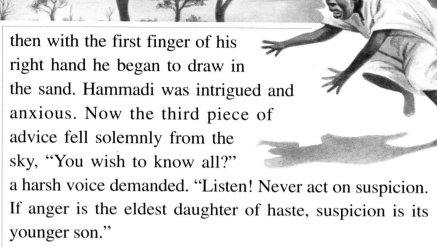

then with the first finger of his right hand he began to draw in the sand. Hammadi was intrigued and anxious. Now the third piece of advice fell solemnly from the sky, "You wish to know all?" a harsh voice demanded. "Listen! Never act on suspicion. If anger is the eldest daughter of haste, suspicion is its younger son."

Hammadi would have liked more advice, but the old man disappointed him. "You have nothing left and I can tell you nothing more. From now on you must find the answers in your own head and heart."

Then the great star began to shine in the sky. The old man went off, driving the three oxen ahead of him with their loads of gold. Hamtudo and Demburu, who up till now had listened, laughed aloud, "Ah! Poor Hammadi, he's tricked you. He's taken the lot! What will you do now?" There was nothing Hammadi could say in reply, but he did not regret what he had done.

A few days later, when the night was wet and stormy, Demburu decided to travel on. A terrible storm broke and he fell, struck by lightning.

People who seek God or wisdom have different ideas from those around them, and often pass for fools.

The star in the story is the one called the *evening star*. To someone who has been taught to understand hidden things, it shows the direction one should take.

Demburu and Hamtudo will pay with their lives for their thoughtlessness.

Hammadi and Hamtudo remembered the first advice the old man had given. They went on their way, very sad at the loss of their friend. They came to the river that formed a frontier between Kaidara's land and the land of people. There they were met by a giant who barred the way. "No man crosses the river unless he crosses in my canoe," he said. "Animals can cross it on foot. Such has been the custom for a thousand years."

Hammadi remembered, "Isn't that the second advice?"

He still had something to pay the ferryman, both for himself and Hamtudo, thanks to the oxen of Demburu. But his friend was obstinate—he did not want to pay or have his friend pay for him. He found a ford and waded in. He took nine steps, but the tenth was fatal! He sank into the water and disappeared forever.

Alone on the bank, Hammadi wept for a long time. At last he climbed into the canoe and crossed the river. He wanted to pay the ferryman but the man refused, took out a big knife, split the boat in two, and left it to sink. He walked on the water as if it were firm ground; when he got to the middle of the river he shouted, "You are wise, Hammadi. You can enjoy all

A river is always the symbol of a difficult or crucial passage. The ancient Greeks believed that people who had died had to cross the river Acheron to reach the underworld. To pass from Kaidara's invisible world to the visible world, one had to cross the river. Hammadi alone would reach the other side.

the gold that's left." Then the mysterious giant turned himself into a whirlwind and dived into the water.

Hammadi fainted, and in a dream he saw again all the events he had lived through since leaving his village. He realized then that this journey had lasted twenty-one years! When he came to, he found all the nine oxen there—Demburu's three, Hamtudo's three, and the three he had given to the old man—his own!

"Really, how lucky I've been," he said to himself. "I have gold to spare! But alas for my poor friends!" And he wept hot tears.

Hammadi marries and has children. He becomes king, loved by all.

Hammadi returned to his village. He married and had many children. But one day he heard a rumor that made him suspicious: "Your wife is seeing another man. Is she unfaithful to you?" He felt so angry he swore to kill any man who dared to come near his dwelling. He unsheathed his dagger, and just as he was about to strike, he heard a shout. The voice was like the voice of the old man in Kaidara's land. "Beware! Suspicion! Never act on suspicion." Hammadi understood at once and put away his dagger.

Marriage in this traditional African society unites two families, two clans. Parents are involved in all the preparations. The ideal number of children is twelve: seven boys and five girls.

When the king died, his people shouted as one: "Hammadi for king!" And Hammadi became a great king, loved by his subjects. But he was not satisfied. He still didn't have the key to the secrets of Kaidara's land. He spent much gold consulting seers, but was none the wiser.

One day an old beggar came to his palace. The king ordered that the strange visitor be brought to him.

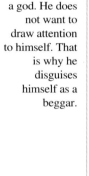

It is not easy to recognize the presence of a god. He does not want to draw attention to himself. That is why he disguises himself as a beggar.

"Old man," said Hammadi. "You are not what you appear to be. You who are bowed down with years, tell me, for I am ignorant, the meaning of the signs I saw in the pygmy-genies' land."

Together they went over the nine signs. "The chameleon changes color according to where it is," said the old man. "That means that you have to adapt to others' ways, be patient and tactful. But also you must not be a hypocrite or unreliable.

"The bat can see at night, but is blind by day. This means that you need clear, penetrating vision in the face of problems, but you must also keep your eyes open to the obvious.

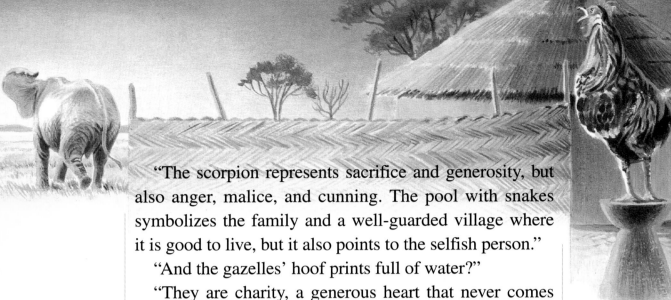

"The scorpion represents sacrifice and generosity, but also anger, malice, and cunning. The pool with snakes symbolizes the family and a well-guarded village where it is good to live, but it also points to the selfish person."

"And the gazelles' hoof prints full of water?"

"They are charity, a generous heart that never comes empty-handed. As for the sixth sign, two trees which dress in the leaves of the other, they suggest death and life, misfortune and happiness, the opposites that follow each other," said the old man.

"The seventh sign, the rooster, represents anger. It is the preferred sacrifice to idols, because it can terrify the mighty elephant, and its crowing chases night away."

"And what about the two springs whose waters mingle above another that is dry?"

The old man smiled. "That means we must communicate. It also means rich people share things with each other and poor people die wretched."

They came to the ninth and final sign, the one of the man who couldn't lift his load. "Great king!" said the beggar, "This sign reminds us that people, even the most

The rooster is often the victim in sacrifices. Afterwards its feathers are stuck to the altar of the ancestors.

At last Kaidara reveals the secrets of wisdom!

illustrious, can be stupid. They think they are powerful, yet they do everything wrong." And the old man added, "Now you know all the signs."

"Who are you?" asked Hammadi, intrigued. "How can I please you and have your blessing?"

"Kaidara gave you gold to open the doors of happiness or unhappiness," was all he replied.

Hammadi asked again, "Who are you?"

"I was close when you met the chameleon, the bat, the scorpion—every time you saw a sign. Your companions chose power and riches. But you took my advice."

"What is your name?" insisted Hammadi.

"I am the one who knows," said the old man. "I am the river, the spring, the town one can never reach . . ." As he spoke he changed into a being of pure light, different from people, animals, plants, trees, and all that exists. Then he spread gilded wings and rose into the sky.

"I am Kaidara," he cried. He flew higher and higher, leaving Hammadi stretched out on the ground, overwhelmed with joy, silence, and wisdom.

That is the end of the tale
of the secrets of Kaidara,
who is far away and close at hand.

THE PLACE OF STORIES IN AFRICAN TRADITION

African ethnic groups.

The teller would remember his story by using a memory aid in the form of a wooden spatula on which he drew the main events.

Kaidara's land is filled with tall grasses, dunes, and endless mirages; skeletal bushes dot the ochre landscape, where strange animals roam.

An ethnic group is a human community having one language, one culture, and shared customs.

Hamadu Hampate Ba, poet and sage of Mali, has written two versions of this story, one in prose and one in verse.

The art of the storyteller

An African story is a landscape with many paths of adventure. As you read the story, you travel on a magic carpet, floating above reality, seeing into its mysteries.

Except at times of sowing or harvest, stories are told in the evening in the pleasant hours after work, when the air is fresh but the golden sand or laterite rock still gives off heat.

Before writing existed, storytellers, as heirs and guardians of the ancestors' memory, were very important. It was their duty to be faithful to customs and traditions, respecting the stories' value as education. But storytellers could be as free as they liked with the text, adapting it according to place and circumstances.

The stories were rich in proverbs, sayings, and humor and would be accompanied by the zither or another instrument, depending on the local custom.

The secrets of Kaidara

Our tale of Kaidara belongs to a type of literature called *jantol,* which is specific to the Peuls. It is a moral and philosophical story, aimed at educated listeners. The story seems to be a fairy tale, but demands sustained attention. Listeners are expected to meditate afterwards to find its deeper meaning.

The *jantol* reminds adults and teaches younger people about the significance of initiation ceremonies (see pages 34–35). It retraces the steps adolescents must take to reach adult status in African society.

INITIATION RITES

Adolescents are asked to endure painful ordeals: being stung by ants or wasps, whipping, mutilation, tattooing on the nape of the neck.

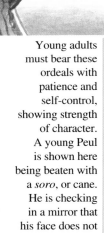

Young adults must bear these ordeals with patience and self-control, showing strength of character. A young Peul is shown here being beaten with a *soro*, or cane. He is checking in a mirror that his face does not reveal the pain he feels.

From childhood to adulthood

Only after undergoing a series of trials, which vary according to the tribal community does a young African become a full member of the village. The child submits to certain rituals, which often take place in the "sacred wood." These rituals evoke death and rebirth: the death of the child and his or her rebirth as an adult.

Such trials are called initiation rites. They give access to a fund of knowledge. The children, grouped by age, spend time away from home, being instructed by the elders of the community in moral, social, sexual, and religious matters, to equip them to become full members of the village.

Three boys seeking knowledge

The episodes experienced by Hammadi, Hamtudo, and Demburu in the story symbolize the trials they must endure if they are to take their place in society.

The first stage is a descent into the bowels of the earth; obstacles and strange encounters punctuate their progress. They must pass through these stages with obedience and trust: all questions are left unanswered. The three children receive oxen loaded with gold.

The second part of the story describes their return journey and its trials. The gold turns the heads of two of the boys. Hammadi alone will discover that material riches are not true wealth, and only he will use the gold to learn wisdom. He will be a powerful king and will not be trapped into a life of ease. In the end Kaidara will reveal to

Circumcision for boys and excision for girls may form part of the rites of passage. These procedures symbolize separation of a person from childhood, with its ignorance and irresponsible behavior.

Young people remain under the tutelage of their elders, particularly for work. Below, a young child from the Cameroons dressed for the circumcision ceremony.

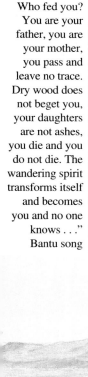

him the true joys of knowledge.

Death rites

Death and the funerals that follow are also rites of initiation, marking the passage from one stage of life to the next.

They are occasions for grand ceremonies—the whole village gathers together for up to ten days. A Peul saying has it that the funeral ceremonies would last forty days for the death of a man more than 105, or for an ox more than 21 years old!

Between the human and the divine

Death is the moment when a unique bond is made with the divine. When one of the Yoruba tribe of the Niger dies, they select a community member to represent the deceased, as though he or she were still alive. Masked and wearing fine clothes, this person reassures people about the deceased's new condition and promises wealth and prosperity to the family.

When the rituals are finished, the deceased joins the ancestors and becomes, in the tradition of many African peoples, a mediator between the living and the gods. The deceased will be celebrated as such on all ritual occasions— invocations, offerings, or initiations that form the rhythm of village life.

Two worlds that must be separate

In some traditions, the young people perform masked dances to console the dead for the life they have lost. The purpose is to help the living to express their grief, and to help the dead to settle peacefully into their new existence by reminding them of important moments in their lives.

Certain ceremonies play an essential role in setting a distance between the worlds of the living and the dead, so that they may not harm each other.

For a while, the dead are considered to be spirits, who may wish the living either good or evil.

"Fire that men watch at night, in the depths of the night—the sorcerer's fire— Where is your father? Where is your mother? Who fed you? You are your father, you are your mother, you pass and leave no trace. Dry wood does not beget you, your daughters are not ashes, you die and you do not die. The wandering spirit transforms itself and becomes you and no one knows . . ."
Bantu song

According to a Sudanese tradition, when someone dies, a close relative, painted with white patterns (the color of death), stands guard to prevent the deceased from trying to return among the living.

In the middle of the page: an animal mask from the Congo. The animal, whose strength is concentrated in its head, confers its own power on the mask that represents it.

Shango, below, god of storms and tempests, is venerated by the Yorubas.

IN THE LAND OF THE GODS

What is animism?

Africans inhabit a world in which nearly everything is sacred, a universe of divinities, genies, and spirits. For Africans, the invisible is as much present as the visible. Illnesses, accidents, births, marriages, and deaths—events of all kinds bring them into contact with the supernatural.

The gods live and manifest themselves in trees, forests, rivers, springs, and animals. They are sacred energies that take their strength from the supreme energy: God. Africa's religious traditions are sometimes known as *animism*. This, however, is only part of the beliefs held in African Religion. Beings are inhabited by spirits (*animus* means spirit) and are given a soul (*anima* means soul).

The supreme being

All beings have come from the same vital principle, the supreme God. This God is sometimes androgy-nous—both masculine and feminine.

In Ghana, some speak of "Father-Mother-God." Generally, the Great God is not often called upon, but is very much present in everyday life. Rain, storms, and sun are attributed to God. For instance, people say, "God is making it hot," instead of "It's hot," or "God is beating the thunder drums," for "It's thundering," or "God has softened the day," instead of "It's nice weather."

A Dogon sorcerer in front of his sanctuary

Baoule statuette from the Ivory Coast representing a spirit (everyone has their own in the next life) and intended to appease its ill will.

Center: a Zairean monkey-fetish holding a bag of magic.

Secondary gods and genies

In various ethnic groups it is said that the Creator, after living on Earth, withdrew to the sky because of people's wickedness. The Creator is presented as an abstract idea rather than as a living person. It is a cosmic force that has a direct effect on the lives of humans.

In most tribes it is neither the origin of good and evil nor the supreme judge. It is without birth and is eternal. It lives in the high places and dominates all.

This force is served by a crowd of secondary gods, genies, and spirits of different ranks and various functions in a complex hierarchy. At the top is a couple, the Great Invisible Ones: the god of water and the goddess of the earth. The first manifests himself everywhere there is water—he is in springs, rivers, wells, ponds . . . and sometimes he takes a human or animal form. He sets rules, like that of not crossing rivers except under certain conditions. Any lack of respect for him can lead to severe punishment, even death. His favors, such as rain, or water in a well, are won by prayers, libations, or sacrifices of chickens, goats, sheep, or other animals.

The earth goddess is the mother goddess, or the goddess of nurture, as in many other civilizations. That is why in certain tribes a woman will eat earth when she is pregnant.

Other gods rank as equals of earth and water. Among the Dogons, the sky and the sun are pitiless rivals. Natural phenomena—thunder, lightning, wind, rainbows—are made into gods because they bring good or inspire fear. Mountains such as Mount Cameroon or Kilimanjaro are formidable gods.

Feared by all, the sorcerer is a person of central importance in the community.

The rainbow is revered and distrusted because of its strangeness. In South Africa, anyone finding themselves where it ends should take to their heels as fast as they can or they will die on the spot. Elsewhere in Africa people avoid pointing at it for fear of having their hand paralyzed.

Antelope mask

Left, the dance of the Ghimbalas in honor of the Niger River, whose spirit enters the dancer.

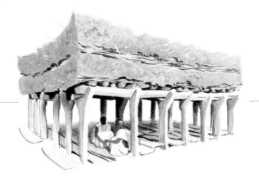

GENIES, SPIRITS, AND ANCESTORS

At the beginning of June, certain tribes in Burkina Faso cover themselves in leaves to celebrate the return of the rains and the sowing season.

The intermediary for the supreme God of the Dogons is the fennec, a desert fox. Seers write their problems in the sand. The tracks the fennec will leave on them during the night will be read as the god's reply (see picture at right).

On the left, the house of palavers, which is where the council of elders gather in the land of the Dogons in Mali.

Below, a Peul herdsman performing the buffalo dance.

A whole population of genies or spirits live on or under the earth, some kindly, others harmful. They appear in the shape of animals but behave like people. They affect everyone's lives. Prayers, offerings, and sacrifices make it possible to avoid their bad deeds or earn their favors. They, too, make rules.

In the depths of the earth live elves who can be heard at night, dancing and laughing.

Remembering the ancestors

The ancestors live in the shadow of the living and are part of the spiritual universe. Some among them are considered divine—such as the founders of families, clans, tribes, or peoples. A common rite is to pray at their tombs to beg for their protection—for health, for crops—and to ask for luck and to be endowed with their strength.

Many Africans arrange a special corner of the courtyard as a shrine for the ancestors —a pile of dry earth, stones, or pottery. On this altar they pour libations, offerings of millet or banana beer. They also place on the altar feathers from the chickens they have offered in sacrifice.

"Listen more often
to things than to beings.
The voice of fire can be heard;
so can the voice of water.
Listen to the bushes
sobbing in the wind:
that is the breath of the ancestors.

Those who have died have not left us,
they are among the shadows that come and go.
The dead are not beneath the ground:
they are in the rustling trees,
they are in the wood that groans,
they are in running water and still water.
They are in the Cave, among the crowds . . .
The dead are not dead at all."

Birago Diop
A 20th-century poet from Senegal

Look for other titles in this series:

I WANT TO TALK TO GOD
A Tale from Islam

CHILDREN OF THE MOON
Yanomami Legends

THE RIVER GODDESS
A Tale from Hinduism

THE PRINCE WHO BECAME A BEGGAR
A Buddhist Tale

I'LL TELL YOU A STORY
Tales from Judaism

SARAH, WHO LOVED LAUGHTER
A Tale from the Bible

JESUS SAT DOWN AND SAID . . .
The Parables of Jesus

DATE DUE